The Seven Gods of Luck

David Kudler ~ *Illustrated by* Linda Finch

Houghton Mifflin Company
Boston 1997

The Seven Gods of Luck is an adaptation of a traditional Japanese folktale.
There are many versions of this folktale but the spirit of the story —
the celebration and generosity of the holiday season — remains the same.

~ ~

For my parents, for my wife, Maura,
and especially for my daughter, Sasha Rachel Kudler — D.K.

For Mom and Dad — L.F.

~ ~

For information about this and other Houghton Mifflin trade and reference
books and multimedia products, visit The Bookstore at
Houghton Mifflin on the World Wide Web at http://www.hmco.com/trade/.

Library of Congress Cataloging-in-Publication Data
Kudler, David.
The Seven Gods of Luck / by David Kudler ; illustrated by Linda Finch.
p. cm.
Summary: Two poor Japanese children hope to be able to celebrate New Year's Day properly,
and because of their kindness and with the help of the Seven Gods of Luck, they are.
ISBN 0-395-78830-7
[1. Seven gods of fortune — Fiction. 2. Brothers and sisters — Fiction. 3. Japan — Fiction.]
I. Finch, Linda, ill. II. Title.
PZ7.K94857Se
1997 [E] — dc20 96-27402 CIP AC

Manufactured in the United States of America
HOR 10 9 8 7 6 5 4 3 2 1

On January first, everyone in Japan celebrates a birthday, no matter when they were born! A great feast is made, with special soups and tasty fish. The favorite dessert is manju, small cakes of sweet rice. The whole festival is celebrated by being thankful for the happiness that has come to you, and by wishing for happiness in the new year. Japanese tradition says that there are seven kinds of happiness; each is represented by one of the Seven Gods of Luck: WISDOM, LONG LIFE, BEAUTY, LAUGH-TER, STRENGTH, HONEST WORK, and PLENTY.

May the Gods of Luck visit you!

Snow is falling
Hail is falling
It just keeps falling
And falling!

Sachiko and Kenji sang as they swept their cottage clean. It was almost New Year's Eve! Just then, their mother came home.

"Mama-san! Mama-san!" said Kenji and Sachiko.

"O-Shogatsu," said their mother, wishing each a happy new year.

"Mama-san, did you bring home the rice for the rice cakes? And the black beans? And the potatoes and radishes for the New Year's soup?"

"Oh, dear ones," said their mother, "there will be no New Year's feast for us this year. To pay off our debts, I had to use all the money we had. There wasn't even enough to buy rice for the rice cakes."

Sachiko and Kenji sat sadly as their mother went to light the small fire. Then Sachiko had an idea.

"I made some beautiful hairpins. Maybe I could go into town and sell them so we can buy rice!"

"And I could come along," said Kenji, "and sell the painted chopsticks I made. I bet they make more money than your hairpins."

"Bet not!"

"Come on, I'll race you!"

Off they went through the snow, until they came upon the shrine of the Seven Gods of Luck. Snow piled up on the stomach of the God of Laughter. It powdered the hair of the Goddess of Beauty and hid the rice sack of the God of Plenty.

"How can they help people get luck, when they're all covered in snow?" said Sachiko.

"Let's brush them off, so they can be nice and clean for the new year," said Kenji.

Sachiko and Kenji brushed the snow off the shoulders of the God of Honest Work, cleared snow from the high forehead of the God of Wisdom, and dusted snow out of the beard of the God of Long Life. When the snow was gone, Sachiko and Kenji bowed to the statues and asked their blessing.

"Give us luck," said Sachiko. "We're off to the town to earn money for our New Year's feast."

"Give us luck so we can start the year in the proper way," added Kenji.

The town was full of people getting ready for the New Year's celebration. People buying food, paying off debts, delivering gifts — running, running, running!

Kenji and Sachiko stood in the snow, trying to get the busy people to buy what they had made, but nobody stopped.

As the sun began to set, they were still there. "Not a single sale and I'm cold," said Kenji.

Sachiko said, "Look at that poor old hat-seller. He looks frozen. He should be home with his family."

Kenji went up to the old man. "Let's trade. Give us those six bamboo hats and you can take what we made. At least then we'll all go home with something different than what we came with."

And so they did. "O-Shogatsu!" said the old man.

"Happy New Year to you, too," said Sachiko and Kenji as they headed home.

When Kenji and Sachiko came to the shrine, the statues were covered in snow again.

"No wonder we didn't sell anything," said Sachiko. "The snow came right back. The poor Gods must have been too cold to help us!"

"Let's give them our hats, to keep them warm and dry," said Kenji.

After they had put each hat on a stone statue, the statue of
the Goddess of Beauty was still bareheaded.

"Here," said Sachiko, tying her kerchief around the statue's
head. "This will look very lovely on her, don't you think?"

Then they trudged home through the snow, singing.

Snow is falling
  Hail is falling
    It just keeps falling
      And falling!

As they went to bed that night, they heard the big bell in the town ringing out one hundred and eight times, to take away the one hundred and eight cares of humankind.

As the final bell rang, the stone statues opened their eyes.

"Hats!" said the God of Wisdom. "What a brilliant idea!"

"And very becoming, wouldn't you say?" asked the Goddess of Beauty.

"Yes, and very kindly given," said the God of Plenty. "We should repay Sachiko and Kenji for their generosity."

The God of Honest Work agreed with him. "We should bring these two a proper New Year's feast, in return for their helpfulness."

So the God of Plenty brought out New Year's soup, sweet rice cakes, and walnuts, good fish to bring harmony, and black beans for health.

"We should bring the feast in these," said the God of Strength. In his large hands, he held enormous bowls of porcelain and gold.

The God of Long Life stroked his long white beard and nodded. "I have learned that those who give happiness to others, give happiness to themselves as well."

"And they've certainly made us happy, wouldn't you say?" chuckled the God of Laughter.

When morning came on New Year's Day, Mama-san went sadly to warm leftovers over a small fire. Kenji woke giggling.

"What are you laughing at, silly?" asked Sachiko.

"I was dreaming we had a wonderful New Year's meal, with lots of cakes and fish . . ." said Kenji.

"And rice! And nuts!" said Sachiko. "Mmmm. It smells so good!"

"I smell it too!" said Kenji. The two children looked
at each other and ran into the outer room. Their mother
stood in the center of the room, looking puzzled.

"O-Shogatsu, Mama-san!" said the children.

Their mother said nothing, but pointed in front of her.

And there, spread out before them in seven huge golden bowls, was the feast of the Seven Gods of Luck.